Valentine's Crushed

Written by: RyAnn Adams Hall

Illustrated by: Inga Shalvashvili

Copyright © 2014 by RyAnn Adams Hall

All rights reserved. No part of this publication may be reproduced, stored in a retrieval system, or transmitted, in any form or by any means, electronic, photocopying, recording, or otherwise, without the written permission or the author.

I dedicate this book to my nieces Abbie and Shelby for letting me use them to inspire the characters in this book. Also, their love for reading books inspires me to keep on writing books for children.

Chapters

Chapter 1- Last Day of School

Chapter 2- Moving Day

Chapter 3- Unpacking

Chapter 4- Sign Up for School

Chapter 5- 1st Day of School

Chapter 6- 2nd Day of School

Chapter 7- Valentine's Day

Chapter 1-
Last Day of School

As I am standing here early in the morning, waiting on the school bus, I almost start to cry. This is my last day of school here. I feel the cool breeze on my face and listen to the leaves rustling around as I hear the school bus coming down the street. I almost hate to go to school today. I do not want to have to tell all my friends good by forever!

See, my dad's job moved and we have to move with it. Our house has already sold and dad bought us a new one. This weekend, I will have to say good bye to the only place I have ever lived.

The bus stops just before me and I wait as the door opens. I get on the bus and sit down with my friends that almost immediately start to cry.

"Oh Abbie, we will miss you terribly!" They all tell me.

"Please don't cry it will only make us all even sadder! I will call and write; everything will be alright."

I tell them trying to make them feel better; even though I know things will never be the same again.

Another thing that is bothering me is that next week is Valentine's Day. I will probably be the only kid in school that won't get a Valentine! No one will know me yet!

When the school bus stops in front of the school and opens the door, we all get off the bus and head inside. All day long, my friends try not to cry. The teachers are making it even worse by informing all the other kids in my classes that it is my last day of school here! My teachers all tell me that they will miss having me in their classes and tell me good luck at my new school.

New School!!

The thought of that is so terrifying. I worry about things like, "What if no one likes me?"

"What if I never find any new friends?"

"Will kids at my new school like the same kinds of things as the kids in my old school?"

"Will I even fit in?"

As school ends, I make sure to hug all my friends' good bye as I head to the bus. This is the last time I ride this bus, with my friends on it, home from school!

As soon as we get to my house, I see the moving truck backed up to the door and boxes going on it. The bus stops in front of my house, I tell everyone good bye, and get off the bus. I stand there and watch the door close and the bus drive off. I start to cry!

I do not want to turn around and see all those boxes going onto the truck. I take a deep breath and try to wipe away the tears. As soon as I am able to hold the tears in, I turn around and head for the house. Mom greets me at the door and hugs me. She tries to reassure me that everything will be alright.

That is one thing about mommas; you cannot get anything past them! She knew I was crying and tried to comfort me. First thing tomorrow morning, we will be heading to the new house, in the new town!

"Where's Shelby?" I ask mom. She's my little sister.

"She's in her room packing up the rest of her toys," says mom. "You should finish packing too. Just leave out an outfit for tomorrow."

"Ok mom, I am going to check on Shelby first and then I will get started." So I go up the stairs and stick my head in Shelby's room and she seems fine. She is excited about moving and getting to decorate her new room.

Dad says our rooms are bigger than the ones we have now.

So I head to my room and finish packing. We have to take our beds apart tonight and put everything but the mattress on the truck. Mom tells me we are having pizza tonight since she's already packed up all the dishes.

As we eat dinner, we all decide to put our mattresses in the living room and leave the TV plugged up. As our last night in our old house comes to an end, I did find it to be quite amusing for all of us to be camped out in the living room all night watching movies until we all passed out.

Chapter 2- Moving Day

Dad heads out to get us breakfast on this awful Saturday. I get dressed and put the rest of my things on the moving truck. As we eat breakfast, I ask dad, "Why couldn't we wait until next weekend, after Valentine's Day is over, to move?"

He said he's sorry, but he has to be at work at his new place of work on Monday.

After we eat, we make sure everything's on the truck. We take one last look around the house, checking every closet, every drawer, and every cabinet. I walk outside and take a deep breath. I silently say good bye to the only world I have ever known and get in the car with mom.

After a couple of silent hours in the car, we pull up to the new house. Although it is larger and nicer than our old one, it still won't ever be the same. Dad gives us a tour of the new house before we start unloading the truck. We head through the living room, the kitchen, the dining room, and then head upstairs.

We look at mom and dad's room, then Shelby's, mine, and mom and dad's new office.

Time to start unloading the truck! Shelby and I may be small, but there are some things we can get off the truck to help out mom and dad. See, I am ten and Shelby is eight years old.

When Shelby and I are out of things to carry, we head to our rooms and start unpacking our stuff. I open up one box that is full of pictures of my friends and my eyes start to fill up with tears again.

After dad comes in to put my mirror on top of my dresser, I start to hang up pictures of my friends on it. This is the only way I will be able to see them every day anymore!

The rest of the day is spent unloading the truck. When it is time for dinner, dad runs to get take-out again. After we eat, dad puts Shelby's and my bed together hoping that we sleep good tonight in our new house.

When dad is done with our beds, he hooks up the TV in the living room so we can watch a movie together before we all head to bed.

When the movie goes off we all give hugs and kisses and head to bed.

I go to my room, but don't shut the door all the way. I cut off the light and lie down in my bed, in my new room!

My new room!

Scary!

I try to figure out what every sound I hear is or I will never be able to sleep. It is scary being in a new home, in a new room, and it is dark!

I keep telling myself that there is nothing to be scared of; it is just a new house! I finally fall asleep and do not wake up until morning.

Chapter 3- Unpacking

"More unpacking to do today!" dad tells us as he heads out to go get breakfast.

"We will go grocery shopping in a little while," mom tells me.

I help her start unpacking the kitchen stuff so she will be able to cook dinner tonight. I am trying to keep myself busy. I almost cry every time I start to think about my friends. And the fact that I am going to feel so sad in a couple of days when I am the only student that won't get a Valentine's isn't helping any.

As soon as dad gets back, we all sit down and eat. After we eat, Shelby and I run upstairs to get out of our pajamas.

I am ready to go to the store so I can see more of what our new town looks like. I sure hope there is something for Shelby and I to do around here.

After dad gets back, we all eat and get ready to go. We all get in the car and head to town.

Wow!
It is Huge!!

I did not realize we are so close to a huge city! I would say that there are plenty of things to do around here for sure!

Dad drives around the city for a while, giving us the Grand Tour! I feel my eyes light up as I look at all the Huge Buildings! They are so neat!

We get to the mall. It is also huge and has a movie theatre in it! A person could spend hours in this mall! We eventually make our way back to the grocery store and then head home to unload the car.

When we get all the food put away, mom tells Shelby and me, "I am taking you girls to sign up for school tomorrow!"

It felt like my heart was going to stop beating! I am so nervous and scared that no one will like me or want to be my friend!

Shelby and I decide to go to our rooms to work on decorating them some more until dinner time. "I'll race you!" Shelby says.

I agree and we run up the stairs as fast as we can! Shelby gets up the stairs first and we start laughing as we head to our rooms.

I open a box that is full of jackets and then I look for some coat hangers. I start hanging up the jackets in my closet. Then I find a box of books and start stacking them neatly on my bookshelf.

Mom comes to my room and asks me, "Do you want to come help me make dinner?"

"I sure do! I love learning how to cook!" I follow her downstairs and together we make dinner. Since I helped cook, Shelby has to help do the dishes!

After dinner, we all get ready for bed. Mom makes a couple bags of popcorns and we all watch a movie together. Dad heads to bed after the movie since he has to work tomorrow.

I go to my room and flip through my photo albums. I miss my friends so much already! I wish I were going to my old school tomorrow. I do not want to go to a new school!

I shut the photo album and set it on the table beside my bed. I decide to go ahead and go to bed before I start crying again.

I get up and crack my door open again. I hope I get used to my new room soon so I won't have to do that anymore!

I cut off the light and lie down. I try really hard to find something else to think about, but when I close my eyes, the tears start coming out. I fall asleep missing my friends so much!

Chapter 4- Sign up For School

Today is the day mom is taking us to sign up for school. I try to lie in bed as long as possible because I am too scared to go!

Shelby, however, is excited to get to go to a new school. She runs in my room and tells me to get up! I really don't want to get out of bed!

When I do finally get up and get dressed, I eat breakfast as mom finds all the paper work she needs to sign us up. As soon as I am done eating, we head for the school!

New School!!!

Oh wow, my stomach is hurting now! I am so nervous!

We get to the school and head to the office. Mom gets us signed up and the principle gives us a tour of the school. She shows both of us where our classrooms are. Then she pulls our teachers out so we can meet them.

When we are done at school, mom surprises us by telling us that she is taking us to the mall. She is going to buy us a new outfit to wear to school tomorrow!

I am so excited now to get to check out our new huge mall! We pull up in the mall parking lot and all I can think is Wow! We get out of the car and head inside!

The mall goes around in a huge oval! The food court is in the middle and the movie theatre is at one end. We walk around the whole mall, stopping at the kids clothing stores.

Shelby and I both get a pair of jeans and a new shirt. We stop at the food court to get some pizza and a drink.

Mom asks us, "Do you girls want to see a movie before we go home?"

"I sure do!" Shelby says excitedly grinning from ear to ear.

"I do too!" I tell mom.

We finish eating and head to the movie theatre. We find a 3-D movie, get our tickets and 3-D glasses, and head inside.

We get some popcorn and a drink, and go find our theatre. We find a seat in the back row. We watch the movie and it looks like every think is jumping out at us! It is so much fun!

After the movie is over, we head home. When we get home, mom starts dinner. Shelby and I go put our new clothes in our room.

I call a few of my friends to check on them and see if I have missed anything. They all tell me that they miss me, but I have not missed anything fun yet.

When mom hollers, "Dinner is done," I make my way down stairs to eat. Dad tells us, "Good luck at our new school tomorrow."

I just smile and say, "Thanks."

I didn't tell dad what I wanted to tell him! "I do not want to go!"

"I am terrified!"

"I am too scared to try new things or places!"

After I eat, I go back upstairs to take a shower and get ready for bed. I cut off the light and lie down. I am too scared to sleep!

I lie here for a very long time staring up at the ceiling! I am going to be so tired tomorrow! I finally fall asleep and do not wake up until morning!

Chapter 5-
1st Day of School

This morning when I wake up, I try to think of a way to get out of going to school.

"I have a fever?" maybe!

"I fell out of bed and broke my leg?" maybe!

"I lost my voice and cannot talk to my new teachers!" maybe!

Although all those stories are believable, I just do not think that mom would believe me!

I get up to put my new outfit on and make my way downstairs for breakfast. Shelby is already eating. I am so glad that she will be going to the same school as me!

See, where we used to live, I was already in middle school. My new school is still in Elementary school.

After we eat, we bundle up, grab our book bags, and go wait for the bus. It is so cold out here! I am so ready for spring time!

Shelby says, "I hear the bus coming!"

I grab her hand and take a deep breath! The bus stops in front of us and we get on it. We find a seat together and head for school.

When the bus drops us off at school, Shelby and I walk inside together. I tell her, "I will see you later on the bus!"

She tells me, "Ok, and do not be scared! It will be alright!"

I find my classroom and go inside. The teacher tells me where to sit, so I go sit down. Of course, after the bell rings, she had to tell the whole class my name and that I am a new student!

I could have melted away! I was so embarrassed! I was surprised when all the kids smiled and said, "Hello!"

The teacher gave me my books and went on with class.

When it is time for lunch, a girl comes over to me and says, "Hello, I am Stacy. Do you want to sit with me and my friends?"

"I sure do! Thank you!" I tell her and I eat lunch with her and her friends Jessica, Sarah, and Danielle.

I walk back to class with Stacy after lunch. I am so glad I did not have to eat alone on my first day here!

After school, I walk to the bus stop and find Shelby. We get on the bus and sit together. She asks me, "So, how was your first day?"

"I tell her, "A lot better than I thought it would be! I did not even have to sit alone at lunch!"

Shelby tells me, "That is good! I told you it would not be as bad as you thought it would be!"

The rest of the way home, Shelby tells me all about her first day. She tells me how many new friends she has and how much fun she had today! I am so happy for her!

When the bus stops in front of our house, we get off the bus and Shelby runs inside! She is excited to tell mom all about her first day!

I wait until Shelby is done to tell mom that it was not as bad as I thought it would be.

Then I head upstairs to call my old friends and do my homework.

Eventually we all eat dinner, take showers, and head to bed. I hope tomorrow is even better than today!

Chapter 6-
2nd Day of School

Today I wake up and get out of bed. I get ready for school and head to the kitchen to eat breakfast. When Shelby and I are done eating, we grab our book bags and head out the door to wait for the bus.

None of our new friends ride our bus, so we still sit together on the way to school.

When we get to school, we tell each other, "See you later!" and we head to class.

After the teacher is done taking attendance, she tells us that we will be making boxes to put our Valentine's in tomorrow.

She picks up a bag off the floor and starts passing out boxes for us to decorate. Then she grabs another bag and puts everything we will need to decorate them on a table. She has paper, markers, glitter glue, you name it!

I love this part of Valentine's Day! I thought to myself. When I get to the table, I pick out pink and purple paper and glitter to do my box in. I hope I at least get one Valentine tomorrow, or I'll be so sad. I will feel like I sat here and made this pretty box for nothing!

Everyone finishes their boxes before lunch and helps the teacher clean up the mess. She gives me a list with everyone's name on it before we head to lunch.

I go to lunch with Stacy again. She is so nice! We chow down on pizza today, My Favorite!!

After lunch, we head back to class and do school work the rest of the day.

I find Shelby after school and we ride the bus home together. She tells me all about the Valentine's box she made and I tell her about mine.

When we get home, mom tells us to hop in the car so that we can go pick out Valentine's and candy to give to our class.

Mom says, "Even if you don't know the kids in your class yet, it will still be nice of you to give them a Valentine."

We get to the store and get enough candy for the kids in our classes. Then we pick out Valentine's for them.

I am so glad the teacher gave me a list of names. I do not know all of their names yet.

When we get home, Shelby and I sit at the table and write names on all the cards and tape candy to them. Even though I do not know any of those kids yet, I still have a lot of fun making the Valentine's!

    I have a few extras, so mom lets me mail them to my old friends. I hope they love them!
    After I am done, I go put them in the mailbox, then head upstairs to do my homework.
    After I eat dinner and take a shower, I head to bed. I have a hard time falling asleep tonight. I am so nervous for tomorrow!

Chapter 7- Valentine's Day

Today when I wake up and get out of bed, I head to my closet. I find a pretty red sweater to wear to school today. I finish getting ready for school and head downstairs to eat breakfast.

When Shelby and I are done, we grab our book bags and bags of Valentine's and go outside to wait for the bus.

When I hear it coming down the road, I start to get really nervous again. It feels like the first day, all over again!

Shelby and I get on the bus and sit together. I look at my bag of Valentine's and hope I did not forget anyone. I would feel so bad if I did!

Shelby is really excited and ready to give hers out to all her new friends!

When we get to school, we tell each other, "Bye!" and head to class.

The teacher tells us, "You will not hand out Valentine's until after lunch! I want you to eat some real food before you stuff yourselves full of candy!"

We do our school work and head to lunch. Stacy, Danielle, and Jessica talk about the boys that they have a crush on and hope that they get a Valentine from them!

I have been too worried about making friends to think about a boyfriend!

When lunch is over, we head back to class. The teacher has already put our Valentine's boxes on our desks. She tells us, "Grab your bags and pass out our Valentines! Have fun!"

I nervously grab my bag and think that I am so glad that the teacher had us put our names on them! I walk around the classroom passing out the Valentine's I made. I have not even looked over at my box. I am too scared too!

When my bag is empty, I take a deep breath and turn around to look at my box!

OMG!! It's full!!

Everyone in class must have gotten me one! How sweet!

I start to run to my desk, but do not want to look crazy so I walk to it and take a seat. When everyone is seated, the teacher tells us, "Dig In!"

I go for it! I have a lot of Valentine's! Some say, "Welcome to our school!" and "Nice to meet you!"

All of these Valentine's are so sweet! And to think I was worried for nothing! I smile as I open the rest of them and pop some candy into my mouth!

Before class ends, I decide to do something. Then my legs start shaking and I am not sure if I can even get out of my seat!

I hold my breath for a second, release it, and then take a deep breath. I get up and walk to the teacher's desk to ask her.

She says, "Sure!" She gets the attention of the class for me.

I look at the class and say, "Thank you for all the wonderful Valentine's and for making me feel welcome here!"

They all smile and say, "Your welcome!"

I walk back to my seat and cannot believe that I just did that!

After school, I find Shelby and get on the bus. I tell her all about what I did and show her all my Valentine's. She tells me, "I told you that you were worried for nothing!"

I smile and agree! Then I listen to her talk about her day on the way home.

I guess moving to a new school really is not as bad as I thought it would be!

Other Children's Books by Mrs. Hall

A Swing Set for her Birthday

Caden Loves His Momma

Rylie's New Bike

Shelby Loves Candy

Abbie Goes to the Zoo

Three Little Sisters

Seasons Come, Seasons Go

Butterfly's Big Adventure

Bella Wants to be a Writer

http://ryannhall3691.wix.com/childrens-books#

http://www.facebook.com/ryannadamshall

CPSIA information can be obtained at www.ICGtesting.com
Printed in the USA
BVIW12n1329170116
433246BV00015BA/114